# The Stuck Truck

## By Michelle Reinshuttle

Illustrated by: Casey McKinley

ISBN-13: 978-1530726493
ISBN-10: 1530726492

FOR REAGAN

One winter's morning it started to snow.

Poppi was a big blue truck with a plow attached to his front.
As the snow fell faster it was time to start his hunt.
It was Poppi's job to find the streets that need cleared.
It was for this kind of weather Poppi was best geared.

Poppi drove slowly down the streets, pushing the snow to the side. The cars behind him were so very happy because now they could drive.

Poppi worked hard, he was having a great day.
But the snow kept falling and got harder to move out of the way.
Poppi reached a big hill where the snow had turned to sludge.
He tried the best he could but the snow would not budge.

When Poppi tried to go backwards his wheels spun in the wet snow.
He could not move, he was stuck,  Poppi thought, "Oh no!"
A nearby tiny tractor saw Poppi in trouble.
He drove over to help as he too had a shovel.

"My name is Timmy," the tractor said, "and I'm not as big as you."
"But I can help move the snow if you would like me to."
"Yes please!" Poppi agreed, "I am one stuck truck."
"You being here is surely a stroke of good luck."

Timmy pushed the snow away from Poppi's tires and gave a gentle tap.
It was just the help Poppi needed to get unstuck from the trap.

"Thank you Timmy.  You did it," Poppi said with a coo.
Timmy smiled great big and proclaimed, "I may be small, but I can help too."

Poppi and Timmy worked together the rest of the day.
All the cars driving behind them cheered, "Hip hip hooray!"
And when all the streets are cleared in the end,
Poppi and Timmy will still be good friends.

The Stuck Truck is based on a true story.

This is Michelle's first published book, despite the dozens of books authored throughout her life.  Michelle was inspired by her parents to bring this story to life for her daughter Reagan.

Michelle is originally from Missouri and lives with her husband and daughter.

Made in the USA
Middletown, DE
09 July 2019